The Wroclaw Krasnale Stories

By Jerzy F. Przybylski

PublishAmerica
Baltimore

© 2010 by Jerzy F. Przybylski.
All rights reserved. No part of this book may be reproduced, stored in a retrieval system or transmitted in any form or by any means without the prior written permission of the publishers, except by a reviewer who may quote brief passages in a review to be printed in a newspaper, magazine or journal.

First printing

All characters in this book are fictitious, and any resemblance to real persons, living or dead, is coincidental.

PublishAmerica has allowed this work to remain exactly as the author intended, verbatim, without editorial input.

Hardcover 978-1-4560-2743-8
Softcover 978-1-4489-6101-6
PUBLISHED BY PUBLISHAMERICA, LLLP
www.publishamerica.com
Baltimore

Printed in the United States of America

It is really unknown...

There is a city in a land far away, right in the middle of Europe.

This is a capitol of the Lower Silesia in Poland. The city's name is Wroclaw.

That city in my opinion is the most hidden treasure of Europe. Is over 1000 years old, and in the history change it looks; from Polish, to Czech, to Austrian, to Prussian to German and again Polish. It is a beautiful city on the Odra River, and has over 100 bridges going across many channels of the river.

It has many fairy stories and one of the best I just now discovered is:

The Wroclaw Krasnale Story...

The Papa Krasnal

About 800 years ago a family of Krasnals moved into the city to bring prosperity and harmony to the people living there. To commemorate that event the City placed The Statues of Krasnals all over the town for citizens and tourist to find and see, enjoy and read about them and in some cases to bring luck to some.

1. The Kissing Pair of Krasnals...

Shortly after moving in to the city The Papa Krasnal and His Girlfriend got merry in the Wedding Castle which is still in use for the Wedding ceremonies for many years now and it is just my guess because of The Kissing Pair of Krasnals up front of The Wedding Castle still is brining luck for the couples who are merry in there. Their fame become so great that for couples from other countries the waiting time for the wedding ceremony reaches already over 80 years...well if you are rich there is a way to speed up the ceremony.

The time moved forward the Krasnal family grew rapidly having many sons.
In some point The Papa Krasnal gave each of His sons a task to do.
As the story goes every Krasnal has a special skill and talent to help people in life.
For good or bad each story goes like that... in not necessarily in that particular order.

2. The Musician and His Fan Krasnals...

One day The Musician showed-up on the Rynek (Main Square of the city) and started playing. His music was terrible so people were giving Him money to stop playing but having one loyal Fan He kept playing in some point He accumulated so much money that at some point He become a President of The Sony Records. Giving the Vice President cheer to His brother Fan...as the story goes they are become rich and currently living in Beverly Hills, California. If you are a musician, singer or composer, I strongly advise you to keep the small copy of The Musician and His Fan Statue or picture handy. It is always good to get some help from someone high in the music business.

3. The Wall Making Krasnal...

The city looks great right now, it was not like that after World War II, ruins and destruction everywhere. Thanks to the heroic work of The Wall Making Krasnal all was done in a good and fast way. If it is possible, I advise people in other countries to come to Wroclaw and first hand examine His work. What is more important when all will be done in the city He will be able to go to other countries if they will offer some great contracts.

Please take my advise: If you are in great need for a perfect construction helper, the time is short and the list of the countries and cities is growing fast. Remember that the appointment book of The Wall Making Krasnal is filled up till 2050. So hurry up.

4. The Dumplings Krasnal...

Everybody around the world try at least once The Dumplings. Many nations claim that they develop that gender of food. Well as you all see the only truth is that The Dumplings originated in Wroclaw, Poland, 100's of years ago by The Dumplings Krasnal. To prove that, all I will say is that, many of you test some meat or cheese dumplings, but do all of you know that the best ...heaven in the mouth are dumplings fill up with berries...Strawberry, Blueberry, Raspberry etc. with sour cream and sugar on top. Just try it and you will know the truth. All of that happens because of the work of The Dumplings Krasnal. Come here to Wroclaw...and test the best of the best.

5. The Food Eater Krasnal

As the story goes; The Food Eater Krasnal duties was to test all the food which was cooked for the large family of Krasnals. In time His name becomes known all over the World and He become a patron of Good Food. As you know many of us before going to the restaurant pray to God to make sure that we will not be sick after. Well my advice to all of you is to Please stop bothering God, He is really extremely busy fixing the huge problems of today world. Please make a short prayer to The Food Eater Krasnal and He will make sure that nobody will be sick after eating in the restaurant, but make sure that the prayer is short and to the point. One day a tour from the USA come to Wroclaw. I guess they prayed too long and Krasnal gave them to much blessings or something...the truth is that when they come back to the USA they became fat...well I hear that obesity in the USA is spreading up in alarming speed. Remember. Pray to The Food Eater Krasnal but make it short to avoid complications.

6. The Syzyfki Krasnale

Did you all experience that feeling...anything you do makes no sense and is repeating it self...well all started in Wroclaw many years ago. The Papa Krasnal gave an order to his two sons to dig out the storage ditch. The work went smooth but The Krasnale were working too close to the Odra river banks, in some point the water from the river came to the ditch and anything they did they never was able to take out all the water. Any parent will be a little angry with a situation like that, so as a punishment for them The Papa Krasnal made a granite ball, He gave to them to push...which till now they are still pushing it back and forth.

Do not be like them...and if you are. try to change....

7. The Love Krasnal

This is the good one. The Love Krasnal, the one who will bring love, happiness in everyone life. He is holding in his hand a heart with the Wroclaw Coat of Arms, He will gave it to anybody who will visit the city and is a good person at heart. As a proof, I will tell You a story. it goes like that…one boy fell in love with a girl far away, she was not 100% sure what to do with him…after visiting Wroclaw and paying respect to The Love Krasnal, she is in deep love now…and I tell you a secret…they will live together soon…

8. The Happiness Giving Krasnal

I know that we all like to be happy, to smile, to have sunshine everyday for their whole lives. At the same time we also know that in life sadness and tears are chasing us often. The good news is that there is a way to get a little help from The Happiness Giving Krasnal. The best way to do that is to get His small statuette or a picture and always keep that close to the heart. In time a person who takes my advice will see the changes at first slow and later at a much faster rate. Well in no time all of you will have a good happy life with a smile on your face. The only way to find out if this is the truth... Please try it...

Jerzy F. Przybylski

The Papa Krasnal

The Kissing Pair of Krasnals

The Musician and His Fan Krasnal

The Wall Making Krasnal

The Dumplings Krasnal

The Food Eater Krasnal

The Syzyfki Krasnale

The Happiness Giver Krasnal

The Lucky Seven Krasnal

The Gambling Krasnals

The Iron Worker Krasnal

The Jail Krasnal

The Traveler Krasnal

The Mail Man Krasnal

The Sleeping Krasnal

The Snoring Krasnal

The Grunwald Krasnal

The Guard Krasnal

The Post Climber
Krasnal # 1

The Post Climber Krasnal # 2

The Golf Players Krasnale

The PRL Krasnal   The Pigeon Lover Krasnal

Author in front of the St. John Cathedral in Wroclaw

9. The Lucky Seven Krasnal

This is one Very Special Krasnal, The Lucky Seven ...I was never lucky in my life like many other people. Yes I was jealous when other people won something in the lottery, casino slot machines or scratches. One day walking on the streets of Old Town in Wroclaw I found Him...well soon after I got myself a post card with his picture...the luck changed for the better at least it looks that way. My recommendation to all of you is...take three of His cards if it is possible. That will bring you luck. After all 3 x 7 = 21...this is a lucky number and on top of that it is supported by The Lucky Seven Krasnal.

10. The Gambling Krasnals

Everyone thinks that card gambling started in Las Vegas, USA about 100 years ago. How wrong they are. Many years ago it all started up on the Salt Square in Wroclaw. The Gambling Krasnals made the Black Jack, Poker etc. games, a money making machine. Many people lost a lot of wealth, few become rich. The richest of them all are The Gambling Krasnals, their fame is so huge that about 20 years ago a delegation of the American Indians came to town to ask for advice. The last time I heard that The Gambling Krasnals were helping the Indians to make money from the games. Of coarse The Krasnals got a great chunk of the money in the process. If anybody would like to see how He live, just go and visit his houses in New York, Hollywood, Monaco, Macao and others places.

11. The Iron Worker Krasnal

He is one of the oldest sons of The Papa Krasnal and because of that He got the hardest duty of them all, He is an Iron Worker, which makes all necessary equipment and tools from iron and other metals. When He was not busy in His spare time He also makes gold and silver jewelry. In the old days most of His work was concentrating to make construction equipment and also home appliances...too bad that not too long ago a President of China visiting Wroclaw offered Him a huge contract so He moved to Bejging where He helped to establish steel mills, and other heavy industry. I heard that He has a lot of respect in there and because of His dedication to hard work He is now a high ranking Communist Party Member... psssss last time I heard, He got a promotion to the Peoples Republic of China Communist Party Politburo.

12. The Jail Krasnal

As in any family with a lot of kids, there are some good kids and a bad one too. The Krasnals family was not an exception to the rules. The Jail Krasnal always was looking for trouble and was making life miserable for the whole city. After the flood in 1996 when He clogged one of the canals of The Odra river which caused the flood, The Papa Krasnal put Him in jail for the next 1000 years...well the situation is that; because there are they still some problems in the Wroclaw which cause hardships for the citizens of the city ...The big question is: Who makes the trouble...

13. The Traveler Krasnal

OOOOOOOOO Boy. We all love to travel, too see the lands far away, different cultures and way of living. The Traveler Krasnal started the hunger for travel. He never stay in one place more than one week, because of His heavy travel schedule He is very hard to be seen in Wroclaw. The legend say that in His life He already been 150 times around the world. I always like to know haw He was able to do that. the gasoline and other fuels are sky high and also plane tickets and so for.

14. The Mail Man Krasnal

We all use Postal Service. in some countries they call it Snail Mail. Did You know that all started in Wroclaw when to celebrate birth of His Second son The Papa Krasnal was sending the invitations to His friends....what He did, He wrote the letters to everybody He knows and His First Born Son deliver them using for the first time The Pony Express, well not all invitations reach the destination, some of them are still on the way.

Any haw for good or bad but from this moment a Post Office was establish... well we all still using it today.

15. The Sleeping Krasnal

It is not supposed to be like that. As a young Krasnal, He was a full of energy and happiness. Something happened later in His life. Nobody knows exactly what but the gossip says that The Sleeping Krasnal started thinking a lot about war and peace and the whole world situation. For many years now the whole world is not a peace full place, He became so depressed, that finally He made a decision to sleep till peace would be universal all over the globe. Last time He was seen sleeping in 1939 on Maginot Defense Line in France when World War II began.

In my opinion He will be sleeping for a long time, well we all hope that one day He will get up and help us all.

16. The Snoring Krasnal

The legend says that because of His snoring one day in 1241 He woke up the whole Army to fight the Mongolian invasion. The European United force lost the battle but the losses of the Mongols were so great that they changed the invasion road and Lower Silesia and Western Europe were safe. Because of that He still is deep in the hearts of the people. Too bad that in His private life, He has been divorced many times because of His snoring.

17. The Grunwald Krasnal

He was a part of the great battle in 1410, on one side the knights of the United Forces of Poland and Latvia and on the other the Teutonic Knights. That was one of the most important battles in Europe, which changed the course of history. The United Forces won the battle. The story says that the The Grunwald Krasnal was credited for killing Urlich von Jungingen, The Grand Master of The Teutonic Knights which ended the battle. Because of that His statue was built in the most visible part of Wroclaw, The Grunwald Square.

18. The Guard Krasnal

He is the most important Krasnal of them all, after of course, the Papa Krasnal. He has a wide variety of duties. He is not only the head of the security forces for the city but also (if someone asks) He will be the guardian for every man or woman who is in love. If you are in need for a great guardian for your girlfriends and boyfriends, husbands and wives, just talk to Him, He never ever let anybody down. He is the most cherished Krasnal in the city and beyond, if someone gets a chance to meet Him

19. The Post Climber Krasnal # 1

Sometimes I'm thinking that life is similar to trying to climb the post hoping that on the top of the post is something worth claiming... well there are many ways to climb the post the easy way or the hard way. I wish that my life had an easy way like The Post Climber Krasnal # 1... look at Him...He is almost on the top and smiling...too bad that I do not have more time to learn something from Him.

20. The Post Climber Krasnal # 2

You see... this is the other way, the hard way to go trough life... I do not think that any of you like to do it that way...too bad that many of us will. The funny part of it is that The Post Climber Krasnal # 2 does that with ease...oooooo look up He also has a smile on His face...

21. The Golf Players Krasnale

Is golf a real sport...some say yes...it must be The Golf Players Krasnale from Wroclaw who developed that game...you do not have to be strong or tall and the money the golf players make is beyond belief...now I know why they came up with a game like that... you see all of them are short and seem not that strong but the happiness is on there's faces telling that they are healthy and rich...well if you all do not trust me on that just look at the sports page in a newspaper...you will see with your own eyes.

22. The PRL Krasnal

He is the youngest son of The Papa Krasnal. In His short life He already experienced a lot:

The rise and fall of The Polish Peoples Republic, (now name of the country changed to The Republic of Poland). He witnessed and has been a part of the great Solidarity movement and because of differences with Lech Walensa, He already retired from public life

Right now He welcomes all the people with an open heart when they visit Wroclaw and if you ask...He will tell you the stories from His life...and believe me you will listen to them with an open mouth.

23. The Pigeon Lover Krasnal

The Pigeon or Dove is a symbol of Peace and prosperity all over The World. This is the reason that The Papa Krasnal ordered His smartest son to be a guardian all of the pigeons.

Did you notice that Pigeons in Wroclaw are friendlier and more beautiful than in other cities... if your answer is yes this is because of a great job of The Pigeon Lover Krasnal. He not only does "The Job"...He also loves them ...well it is possible that in return the pigeons keep peace and prosperity for the city. It just cross my mind. What will happen if we all not only do "The Job" but also put a little heart in to it. Let's try together.

I hope that all of you like The Wroclaw Krasnale Stories...It was my intention to put in a funny way some important historical facts in to them. Yes some of them are fantasy but please read them closely...Who knows, it is possible that some of you will start looking and act differently in your lives. And maybe, just maybe, one day you would like to come to Wroclaw... The Cosmopolitan City in the heart of Europe...You will like the experience... this is a promise.

Jerzy F. Przybylski (ASCAP)

CPSIA information can be obtained at www.ICGtesting.com
Printed in the USA
BVOW072130241011

274432BV00001B/30/P

9 781448 961016